THE MATZAH MAN

A PASSOVER STORY

⌘ ⌘ ⌘

by Naomi Howland

CLARION BOOKS/NEW YORK

Clarion Books
a Houghton Mifflin Company imprint
215 Park Avenue South, New York, NY 10003
Copyright © 2002 by Naomi Howland

The illustrations for this book were executed in gouache
and cut-paper collage with colored pencil.
The text was set in 14.5-point ITC Bookman Light.
Book design by Carol Goldenberg.

Library of Congress Cataloging-in-Publication Data

Howland, Naomi.
The matzah man : a Passover story / Naomi Howland
p. cm
Summary: Just before the Passover seder, a man baked from scraps
of matzo dough escapes from the oven and eludes a number of pursuers
until he meets clever Mendel Fox.
ISBN 0-618-11750-4
[1. Fairy tales. 2. Passover—Fiction. 3. Judaism—Customs and practices—Fiction.
4. Humorous stories.] I. Title.
PZ8+
[E]—dc21   2001028482

TWP 10 9 8 7 6 5 4 3 2 1

In memory of my grandmother, Mildred Spiro

⌘ ⌘ ⌘

INSIDE MR. COHEN'S BAKERY, the racks were filled with Passover matzah. The baker rolled out his last scraps of dough. He added a bit here and a pinch there and shaped a little man. He pricked the dough all over, popped it into the oven, and closed the door.

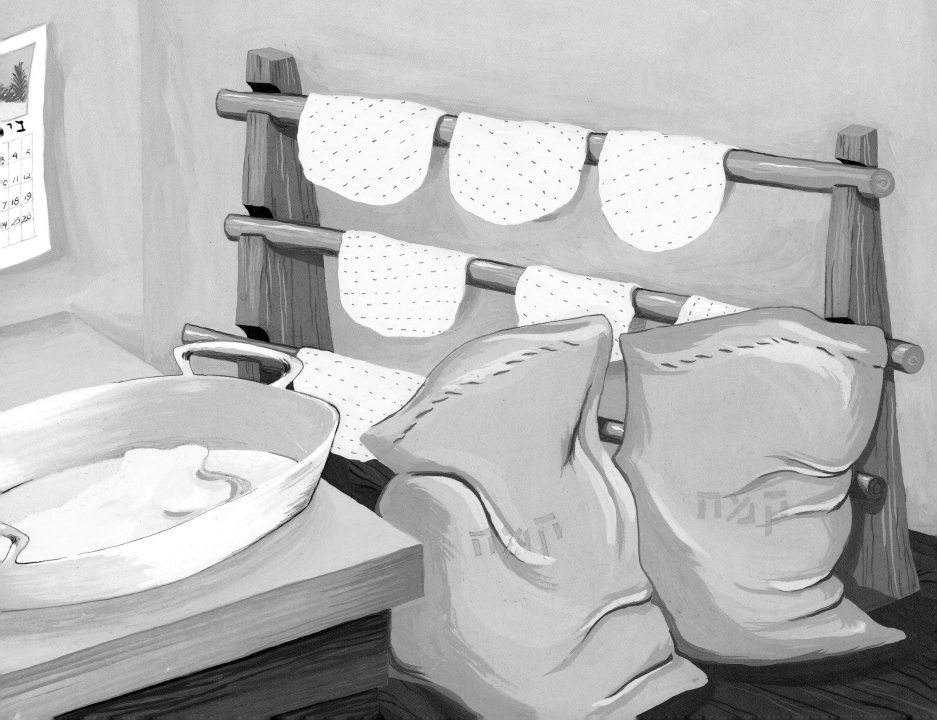

Mr. Cohen was busy cleaning up when suddenly he smelled the matzah, almost burning! He hurried to the oven and opened the door, but the minute he did, that piece of matzah jumped out and said,

Hot from the oven I jumped and ran,
So clever and quick, I'm the Matzah Man!

And off that rascal ran, around the sacks of flour, between the legs of the baker, and right out the door.

"Stop, Matzah Man!" cried Mr. Cohen, and he began to chase the little matzah man.

Through the village they raced. A red hen spied the little matzah man, crisp and crackly, running by.
The matzah man said,

Hot from the oven I jumped and ran,
So clever and quick, I'm the Matzah Man!

"Stop, Matzah Man," clucked the red hen. "You would make a tasty treat for my new chick-chick-chicks."

The little matzah man looked at the red hen, stuck his nose in the air, and said,

I've run from the baker whose matzah is best,
and—
　　　ka-naidle, ka-noodle, ka-noo—
　　　　I'll run away from you, too!

And he went pell-mell over the fence.

Cousin Tillie was sampling her tender Passover brisket when
the toasty little matzah man rushed past her door.
The matzah man teased her, saying,

Hot from the oven I jumped and ran,
So clever and quick, I'm the Matzah Man!

"Stop, Matzah Man," called Cousin Tillie. "You'd be the perfect
mouthful with my delicious brisket."

10

The little matzah man waggled his finger at Cousin Tillie and said,

I've run from the baker whose matzah is best,
and from the red hen who left eggs in her nest,
and—
      ka-naidle, ka-noodle, ka-noo—
         I'll run away from you, too!

And that little scamp raced off down the road.

Auntie Bertha was out shopping in her brand-new shoes. She saw the crunchy matzah man running right toward her.
The matzah man said,

Hot from the oven I jumped and ran,
So clever and quick, I'm the Matzah Man!

"Oh, please stop, Matzah Man," cooed Auntie Bertha. "You would look just adorable on the Passover table."

The little matzah man made a rude face at Auntie Bertha and boasted,

I've run from the baker whose matzah is best,
and from the red hen who left eggs in her nest,
from old Cousin Tillie with brisket-filled pan,
and—
    ka-naidle, ka-noodle, ka-noo—
        I'll run away from you, too!

And he scooted around the corner.

Grandpapa Solly was chopping onions for his special Passover gefilte fish. The onions were making him cry, but he could still see the matzah man through his tears.

The matzah man said,

Hot from the oven I jumped and ran,
So clever and quick, I'm the Matzah Man!

"Stop, Matzah Man," cried Grandpapa Solly. "You'd be a delectable nosh with this gefilte fish."

The little matzah man put his hands on his hips and bragged,

> I've run from the baker whose matzah is best,
> and from the red hen who left eggs in her nest,
> from old Cousin Tillie with brisket-filled pan,
> and big Auntie Bertha, in high heels she ran,
> and—
> > ka-naidle, ka-noodle, ka-noo—
> > I'll run away from you, too!

And he sped across the bridge.

Miss Axelrod was dropping the last matzah ball into her chicken soup when the browned little matzah man ran past. He shouted,

Hot from the oven I jumped and ran,
So clever and quick, I'm the Matzah Man!

The little matzah man had such chutzpah! He said,

I've run from the baker whose matzah is best,
and from the red hen who left eggs in her nest,
from old Cousin Tillie with brisket-filled pan,
and big Auntie Bertha, in high heels she ran,
then Grandpapa Solly, from onions he's crying,
and—
ka-naidle, ka-noodle, ka-noo—
I'll run away from you, too!

And zippity-zip, away he went.

A gray goat was pulling tender young radishes out of the garden when he noticed the tasty little matzah man.

The matzah man stamped his foot and said proudly,

Hot from the oven I jumped and ran,
So clever and quick, I'm the Matzah Man!

"Stop, Matzah Ma-a-a-an," bleated the goat. "I would like to ha-a-a-ave a bite of you."

The little matzah man laughed and said,

I've run from the baker whose matzah is best,
and from the red hen who left eggs in her nest,
from old Cousin Tillie with brisket-filled pan,
and big Auntie Bertha, in high heels she ran,
then Grandpapa Solly, from onions he's crying,
and then from Miss Axelrod, matzah balls flying,
and—
ka-naidle, ka-noodle, ka-noo—
I'll run away from you, too!

And he hurried past the goat.

Just at that moment young Mendel Fox came to the door of his house.

What a commotion!

Mendel saw the little matzah man running down the road, chased by the gray goat, Miss Axelrod, Grandpapa Solly, Auntie Bertha, Cousin Tillie, the red hen, and Mr. Cohen, the baker. The matzah man looked back over his shoulder and panted,

Hot from the oven I jumped and ran,
So clever and quick, I'm the Matzah Man!

"Stop, Matzah Man," Mendel said. "I'll help you. Hide behind me." The matzah man flattened himself behind Mendel.

"They're getting closer!" Mendel shouted. "Hurry, get behind the cushion." The matzah man covered himself with the pillow.

"I can still see you," cried Mendel. "They're coming up the steps! Quick, hide here." The matzah man jumped up on the table and slipped beneath the matzah cover.

Mr. Cohen looked around. "Did you see a little piece of matzah run this way?" he asked.

Mendel shrugged.

Miss Axelrod peeked under the table. The red hen picked up the cushion on Grandpapa Solly's chair. No one could find the Matzah Man. So one by one, the tired guests plopped down in their seats.

"Let's begin the seder," said Mendel. He handed his grandfather the plate of matzah. Grandpapa Solly reached under the matzah cover. Snap! The matzah was broken.

The plate was passed around the table.

"Ta-a-a-asty matzah!" said the gray goat between bites.

Now the horseradish was making Grandpapa Solly cry. He nibbled a piece of matzah. "So crunchy and delicious," he said through his tears.

"The best matzah we ever ate," agreed Cousin Tillie, Auntie Bertha, and Miss Axelrod.

The red hen pecked at her matzah. "Cri-cri-cri-crispy."
Mr. Cohen smiled.
Everybody ate a piece of matzah except Mendel Fox. He had
two pieces. And that was the end of the matzah man!

A PASSOVER GLOSSARY

gefilte fish Ground fish, such as pike, carp, or whitefish, formed into a rounded patty, wrapped with fish skin, and simmered. *Gefilte* (geh-FIL-teh) means "stuffed" in Yiddish. The dish is traditionally served cold, with horseradish.

matzah Flat, crisp, crackerlike bread, the only bread eaten during the eight days of Passover. Thin cakes are formed from flour and water, perforated, and baked. The whole process is completed in eighteen minutes so that the dough does not have time to ferment and rise. *Matzah* (MOT-zuh), also spelled *matzo, matzoh,* or *matza,* is the Hebrew word for "unleavened," and the eating of matzah reminds Jews of their ancestors' hasty flight from slavery in Egypt, when they could not wait for the bread to rise.

matzah balls Dumplings formed from matzah meal (ground matzah), water, and eggs, often served in chicken soup.

matzah cover A special cloth that covers the matzah. As a seder begins, the matzah under the cover is blessed and then broken.

Passover The holiday that celebrates the Israelites' miraculous deliverance from slavery in Egypt more than three thousand years ago. One of the most important holidays in the Jewish calendar, Passover, known as *Pesach* in Hebrew, takes place in March or April and lasts for eight days. The first two evenings of the holiday are observed with a meal called a seder, at which dishes such as gefilte fish, matzah ball soup, and brisket are traditionally served.

seder The Passover meal. At the table, participants follow along in a book called a haggadah (ha-GA-da) as blessings are read, the story of Exodus is told, and symbolic foods such as matzah and bitter herbs are eaten to remind the participants of the Israelites' suffering in Egypt. After the festive meal, the seder concludes with psalms of praise and the singing of songs. The word *seder* (SAY-dur) means "order" in Hebrew. Each chair around the seder table customarily has a cushion on the seat, signifying that those gathered may eat at their ease, unlike their ancestors, who were held in bondage.

Yiddish A language spoken by many Jews. *Chutzpah* (HOOTS-puh, meaning "boldness, nerve") is a Yiddish word.